With love for the three women who
have blessed my life, Sue, Cara, and
Lisa ... it's time for new adventures.

F.F.

PUMPKINVILLE

Written & Illustrated by
Frank Fiorello

First Edition

10 9 8 7 6 5 4 3 2 1

Copyright © 2001 by Frank Fiorello

www.pumpkinpatchbooks.com

Library of Congress
Control Number:
2001117020

Paper Back ISBN:
0-9708400-0-4

Summary:
Peter and his animal friends join forces to grow the biggest pumpkin in PUMPKINVILLE!

Printed in Hong Kong

Far away, deep in the land of orange, surrounded by cornstalks and pumpkin fields, lies a town called PUMPKINVILLE.

So named because the people of PUMPKINVILLE loved pumpkins and the color orange.

In fact, all the
houses in PUMPKINVILLE
were painted orange.

The
citizens
all wore
orange
clothes.

And they even ate
ORANGE food ...
like pumpkin bread,
pumpkin muffins and
pumpkin face cookies.

The people of
PUMPKINVILLE
even ate
pumpkin spaghetti ...

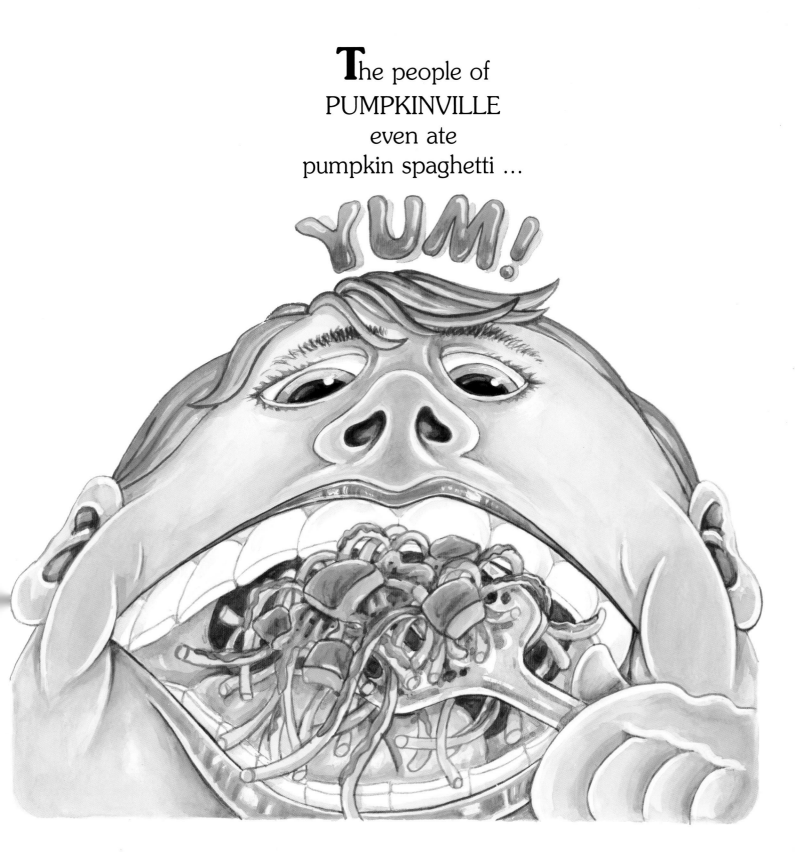

HEAR YE HEAR YE
Citizens of
PUMPKINVILLE
Whoever grows the
Biggest and Brightest
of pumpkins
will be crowned
• GRAND
PUMPKIN
MASTER •
and their giant
pumpkin will lead the
PUMPKINVILLE
parade in autumn

the Mayor

Each year, the mayor of PUMPKINVILLE announced a
Pumpkin Proclamation.

Well, this was great news for a little boy named Peter of PUMPKINVILLE. Peter loved pumpkins, and he knew that he could grow the biggest and brightest of pumpkins.

Everyone said that Peter had an ORANGE thumb.

So Peter of PUMPKINVILLE set out to plant his award-winning pumpkin. First, he found the pouch of magic seeds that he saved from last year's pumpkin.

Peter knew that to grow the largest pumpkin, he would need the help of all his animal friends.

Poncho the donkey would take Peter deep into the forest where the earth was rich and dark ... just right for pumpkin planting.

Gus the goat would
search for twigs and
sticks to make the
perfect skeleton for
pumpkin's body.

Baah the sheep would let Peter trim some of her wool to make a shirt and pants for pumpkin.

Straw for stuffing pumpkin would be gathered by none other than Max the mouse.

Pooch the puppy would be just the right size to sit in pumpkin's head.

And Piggers the pig … well, Piggers was content to lie in the mud and nod her approval of Peter and his friends.

Off to the forest rode Peter of PUMPKINVILLE atop Poncho the donkey, followed by Gus the goat, Baah the sheep, Max the mouse and Pooch the puppy ... as Piggers the pig snorted goodbye.

Soon, Peter found a small clearing in the forest where sunlight and rain and earth would come together to nourish the magic seeds.

Gus the goat scratched at the forest floor, clearing away old decaying leaves.

Next, Poncho kicked up the dirt to make it soft for planting.

Baah nudged the soft dirt into a small hill.

And Max the mouse used his pointed nose to poke holes in the dirt, making room for the pumpkin seeds.

Peter untied his pouch of magic seeds and plucked three plump seeds for planting.

One by one, he gently put the seeds in the holes and covered them lightly with dirt.

"**A**re they growing, yet?" asked Pooch the puppy.

"Not yet," said Peter. "First a little water and then lots of hope and faith that one of the seeds will grow into the biggest and brightest pumpkin of PUMPKINVILLE."

With that said, Peter and his band of pumpkin planters made their way back home to PUMPKINVILLE.

Upon their return, Piggers snorted questions, "How big is the pumpkin? Where is it? Did we win the biggest and brightest pumpkin award?"

"No, no and no!" said Peter. "Pumpkin needs time to sprout and grow."

ack in the forest, those magic seeds began to poke their wee heads out from the hill of soft dirt. The power of earth, sun and rain made a nourishing meal for pumpkin as it grew and grew.

Pumpkin vines traveled along the forest floor, latched onto an old tree and grew upward toward the sky. Soon, pumpkin appeared from the tree top, growing larger and larger.

In the forest, unknown to Peter and his friends, lived a family of three trolls. They did not like pumpkins, especially Peter's pumpkin, growing right above their heads.

The trolls planned to cut down Peter's pumpkin and watch it splatter on the forest floor.

Piggers the pig could see pumpkin growing in the distance.

And he also saw the trolls, who were set on destroying pumpkin.

Piggers snorted, "Peter, come quickly! You must save pumpkin!"

Peter tied a cart filled with straw to Poncho
and off they rode to rescue pumpkin.

The trolls climbed on top of one another, ready to chop down pumpkin.

CHOP! CHOP! CHOP!

Peter and Poncho arrived just in time as pumpkin fell into the straw cart.

"Hurry, Poncho!" shouted Peter.

Poncho leaned his head forward and grit his teeth as smoke poured out of his nostrils.

Clippity clop, clippity clop. Off they went.

Escaping the trolls, Peter and his pumpkin arrived home safely. Now it was time to get pumpkin ready for the autumn parade.

The Mayor of PUMPKINVILLE proclaimed Peter's pumpkin
the biggest and brightest and crowned Peter, the GRAND
PUMPKIN MASTER!

And the little orange town of PUMPKINVILLE cheered as Peter, Poncho, pumpkin and friends strolled down Main Street leading the autumn parade.